Chook Doolan

the newest pet

First published in 2016
by Walker Books Australia Pty Ltd
Locked Bag 22, Newtown
NSW 2042 Australia
www.walkerbooks.com.au

1

National Library of Australia
Cataloguing-in-Publication entry:
Roy, James, 1968– author.
The newest pet / James Roy; illustrator:
Lucinda Gifford.
ISBN: 978 1 922244 94 9 (paperback)
Series: Roy, James, 1968– . Chook Doolan.
For children.
Subjects: Friendship – Juvenile fiction.
Pets – Juvenile fiction.
Other Creators/Contributors: Gifford, Lucinda,
illustrator.
A823.3

The illustrations for this book were created
with brush, pen and ink
Typeset in Bembo Educational and
Love Ya Like A Sister
Printed and bound in Great Britain by Clays
Ltd, St Ives plc

Chook Doolan

the newest pet

story by James Roy and illustrations by Lucinda Gifford

WALKER BOOKS
AND SUBSIDIARIES
LONDON • BOSTON • SYDNEY • AUCKLAND

Chapter 1

Hi. My name is Simon Doolan, but most people call me Chook, which is another name for a chicken.

And that's what I am. I'm a chicken.

I'm not a real chicken – don't be silly. I'm just a boy. A **not-very-brave** boy.

This is **me** with my best friend, **Joe**. I'm the scared-looking one.

I don't think Joe's frightened of anything. Well, maybe maths tests. But I can't think of anything else that scares Joe.

My family has two pets.

This is Flexy-Lexi.

Flexy-Lexi is a cat, in case you couldn't tell.

And this is Bruce.

Bruce and Flexy-Lexi aren't friends. I guess you can work out why.

Bruce is new in our house. My cousin Dee-Dee gave him to me when she moved to Hong Kong.

Bruce lives in a bowl in my bedroom. We talk to each other all the time. He doesn't say very much, mostly because he's a fish.

But he's an excellent listener.

"He's like you, Simon," Dad says. "And the world needs more listeners."

I think Bruce might be pretty brave. When you look at him in his bowl, he comes right over to the glass. If I was living in a glass house in a new place and a giant was staring in at me, I'd probably go and hide behind my fern.

Chapter 2

At school,
Ms Rashid
hands out
notes to the
whole class.

Next Monday is

Bring a Pet to School Day.

This year we are raising money for the Alton Road homeless shelter. Bring your pet along for judging and prizes. Please don't forget leads for dogs, crates for cats and cages for everything else. Remember to get your parents to fill out the permission slip. The entry fee is a gold coin donation.

"I want to bring Bruce, but I don't know if I can," I say to Joe.

"Of course you can," Joe replies. "He's a pet, isn't he?"

"The note says anything other than a dog or a cat has to be in a cage. Fish can't live in a cage. All the water would run out."

Joe smiles. "I think a

fish tank would be okay,"
he says. Then he looks a
bit sad.

"What's wrong?" I ask.

"At least you have a pet to bring. I wish my sister wasn't so allergic. She only has to pat a cat or a dog and she gets all **red** and **spotty**. And **grumpy**."

"You need a pet you can have just for one day," I suggest. "One that doesn't make her spotty."

"What I *really* need is a new sister," Joe sighs.

At dinner, I ask Mum and Dad what they think I should do to help Joe.

"It's not your fault Joe's family doesn't have a pet," says Mum.

"I don't want him to feel left out," I say. "That's awful."

Dad shrugs. "Maybe he'll just have to do without."

"That's no good. Joe hasn't got a pet, and **I'm going to find him**

one. I am! It can't be too scary, though. So spiders, scorpions and most reptiles are out. And guinea pigs."

The next day I try to make Joe feel better.

"Don't worry, you'll think of something," I say. "You always do. You're good at thinking of things."

"Yes, but I'll have to do it soon," Joe says. "Pet Day is only two days away."

Two days? Two days isn't very long!

Chapter 3

That afternoon Joe comes to our house to play after school. He walks home with Ricky and me.

Just as we get to the shops I have what might be an idea. I stop at the corner near Mrs Pho's bakery, and point down the side street. "The pet shop," I say.

"Are you still looking for a pet for Joe?" Ricky asks. "You don't have any money, Chook."

"Maybe they'll let us borrow one."

“That’s the silliest thing you’ve ever said.” Ricky laughs. “Good luck. I’ll see you at home.”

Joe frowns. “I don’t think they’ll let us *borrow* a pet, Chook.”

“Well I’m going to ask,” I say. “Or maybe you can. It’s probably better if you do the asking.”

“Why me?”

I don't want to admit I'm scared, so instead I say, "Because it's your pet."

Joe shrugs. "I think Ricky's right. It sounds like a silly idea."

"Should we just look?"

"Fine." Joe sighs. "Let's look."

The pet shop is only big enough for a couple of puppies, a few canaries and budgies in cages, some tanks of fish and a giant white rabbit with huge floppy ears.

The man behind the counter looks up from his newspaper as we walk in. "Good afternoon," he says. He sounds bored. I'd be bored too, if I had to talk to canaries, fish and a rabbit all day. "How can I help?"

"Um ..." I say.

"We're just looking," says Joe.

"Leave your bags out the front. And no tapping on the fish tanks," the man says.

We wander around the shop. We don't say anything. Each time the man turns a page he glances up at us. He's probably making sure we're not stealing anything.

"Well?" whispers Joe. "Are you going to ask?"

"Ask what?"

"About borrowing a pet."

"Why don't *you* ask him?" I whisper.

"It was your idea."

"It's your pet."

The man clears his throat. "What do you want to know?"

"Um ..." I say again. "Um ..." It's like I've forgotten the right words. It's like I've forgotten *all* words.

"Would we be able to borrow a pet?" Joe asks. "It would be just for one day."

The man laughs and turns another page. "Nice try," he says. "Goodbye, boys."

Chapter 4

Joe and I are having afternoon tea when I notice something at the end of the table.

"Look," I say, picking up the piece of paper. "It's an ad for the animal shelter."

"So? I can't take a pet home."

"Maybe the *shelter* will let you borrow a pet, just for one day."

"Maybe," he says. "It can't be a cat or a dog, though. My sister's allergic, remember?"

"I remember," I say. "If I get the phone, will you talk to them?"

Joe shakes his head.

"*I'll* get the phone, and *you* can talk to them. It's your idea."

"It's your pet."

"Not yet. Seriously, Chook, **don't be such a chicken!**"

Joe passes me the phone and I dial the number. It rings twice before I hang up.

"What's wrong?" Joe asks me.

"No one's there."

"You didn't wait long enough! Do it again."

I dial the number again. This time I let it ring four times, and I'm about to hang up when the phone goes *click*.

"Hello, Animal Rescue Centre," a lady says. "How

can I help you?"

"Oh ... hi," I say.

"Hello. Can I help you?"

"Hi."

"Hello. Can I help you?"

"What animals do you have?" I ask.

"Well, we have all kinds of animals. Cats, dogs–"

"His sister's allergic," I say.

There's a pause.

"Okay. Birds, a few guinea pigs. What are you looking for?"

"Something we can borrow," I say.

"Borrow?" It sounds like the lady's going to laugh. "You can't *borrow* an animal."

I shake my head at Joe. "She says you can't

borrow animals from there," I tell him.

"Hang up!" he says. **"Hang up quick!"**

Chapter 5

It's Pet Day. I'm feeling sad as I walk to school. Joe still doesn't have a pet to bring, and we haven't been able to think of a way to get him one.

Mum has put some plastic wrap over the top of Bruce's bowl to stop the water (and Bruce) splashing out. But I'm still worried.

"Hold on, Bruce," I say. "Sorry about the waves."

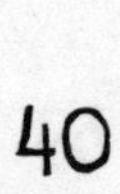

Ricky's walking way ahead of me, as usual. He stops at the corner. "Come on, Chook. Run!" he calls.

"I can't run," I say. "I'll spill Bruce."

"Fish are stupid. Wait! What's this?" Ricky drops his bag and rushes over to a small bush beside the footpath. "Quick, Chook, tip out your lunch. Give me your lunch box."

"No!" I say. "Why?"

Ricky cups his hands around something and walks towards me.

I back away, being careful not to spill Bruce. "What have you got?"

"It's a pet for Joe," Ricky says. "Quick, where's your lunch box?"

"What is it?"

Ricky is really close to me now. He holds up his hands. "It's got lots of legs."

I don't want to squeal, but I can't help it. "What is it?" I ask again.

"Have a look and find out."

"Is it a spider? I'm not putting a spider in my bag!" I shout as I turn and start running. Bruce's water is sloshing about. "Sorry, Bruce."

"It's just a dumb grasshopper," Ricky calls after me. "**Why are you such a chicken, Chook?**"

"I don't know!" I yell. "**I just am!**"

Chapter 6

Our classroom is like a zoo. A noisy, smelly zoo. Or maybe an ark.

Kids have brought cats in crates, rabbits in hutches, birds in cages, guinea pigs in shoeboxes, lizards in plastic containers.

Annie Wong even has a white mouse in a tennis ball tube. (Ms Rashid checks that Annie has made holes in the lid. She has.)

Plus there are all the dogs. Some are bigger than the kids holding onto the leads!

I'm the only person with a fish. And Joe is the only person with no pet at all. He sits at his desk with his chin in his hands. He looks like he's about to cry.

Ms Rashid walks around the classroom collecting permission slips and money. She stops beside Joe's desk.

“Didn’t you bring a pet, Joe?” she asks.

He shakes his head sadly. Then he hands Ms Rashid a gold coin.

“Why are you paying?” I ask him.

“Mum said the homeless shelter is a good cause.”

"Joe,
I think it's
very kind of
you to donate anyway,"
Ms Rashid says as she
moves to the next row.

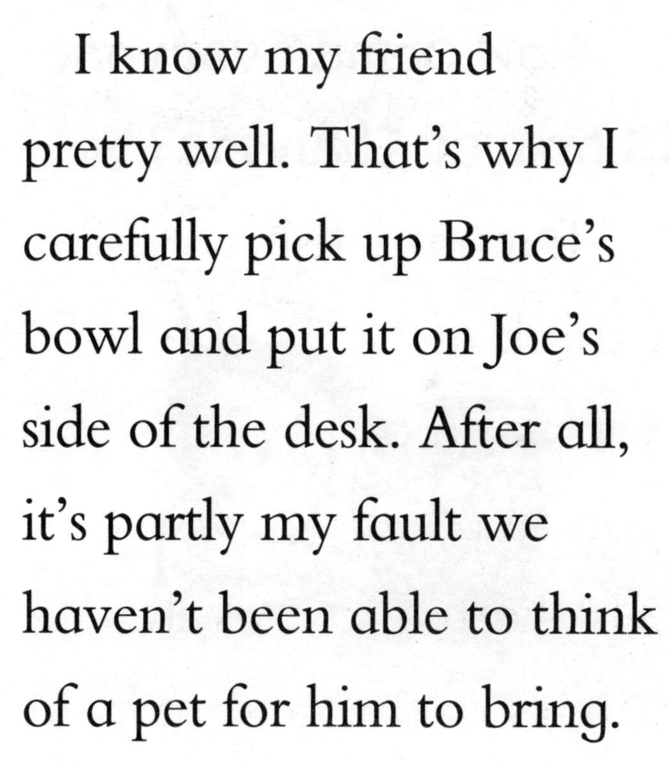

"Would you like to look after Bruce for a while?" I ask.

"I don't care," he says.

I know my friend pretty well. That's why I carefully pick up Bruce's bowl and put it on Joe's side of the desk. After all, it's partly my fault we haven't been able to think of a pet for him to bring.

Joe rests his chin on his folded arms and watches as Bruce swims right over to the glass to say hello.

How come everyone is braver than me?

Even my fish.

Chapter 7

Ms Rashid claps her hands. “All right, class, let’s sit down,” she says. “Wow, look at all these wonderful pets!”

Everyone looks around and smiles. Bruce’s face is still up to the glass.

Even Joe manages a bit of a grin at him.

"Who thinks they've got the oldest pet?" Ms Rashid asks.

A few people raise their hands. After a lot of talk, we decide that Nathan Olivetti's turtle, Mr Snaps, is probably the oldest.

"And who do we think has the *cutest* pet?" Ms Rashid asks.

Now everyone's calling out and arguing. In the end we can't decide between Jamie Alonso's tiny grey kitten and Praj Patel's guinea pig. We call it a draw.

"And who has the youngest pet?"

Suddenly Joe sits up straight. His eyes are wide. He looks very excited about something.

"Chook," he whispers. "Chook! I think we've got the youngest pet *in the world.*"

"Who? Bruce?"

Joe points at Bruce's bowl. "No. Look at this!"

"What is it?"

"Chook, are you sure Bruce is a boy?" Joe asks.

"No, he's a fish," I reply.

"I know, but is he a *boy* fish, or a *girl* fish?"

I shrug. How can you even tell if fish are boys or girls?

"Why?" I ask.

"Because I think your goldfish just laid some eggs."

I bend down to have a closer look.

Floating near the surface of the water are some tiny white dots. Others are caught up under the leaves of Bruce's fern.

"Are you sure they're eggs?"

"I think so," Joe replies. "Can I have one?"

"A fish egg? What for?"

"As a pet," he says.

I think about this. It's probably all right if he has one of Bruce's eggs as a pet. In fact, if Joes likes, he can have all of them!

"Sure," I say. "That might be the best plan ever. What are you going to call them?"

"I haven't decided yet. What are you going to call your fish now?"

"He's already got a name," I say. "It's Bruce."

"Bruce?"

"Yes. His name is Bruce. Remember?"

Joe laughs. "Bruce just had babies. Isn't Bruce a silly name for a girl?"

My name is Simon Doolan.
But you can call me Chook
- almost everyone does.

Chook Doolan is too much of a chicken to walk to school by himself! But then Dad tells him the special "Walking to School" rule. What could go wrong?

ISBN: 978 1 922244 93 2